W9-CFQ-520

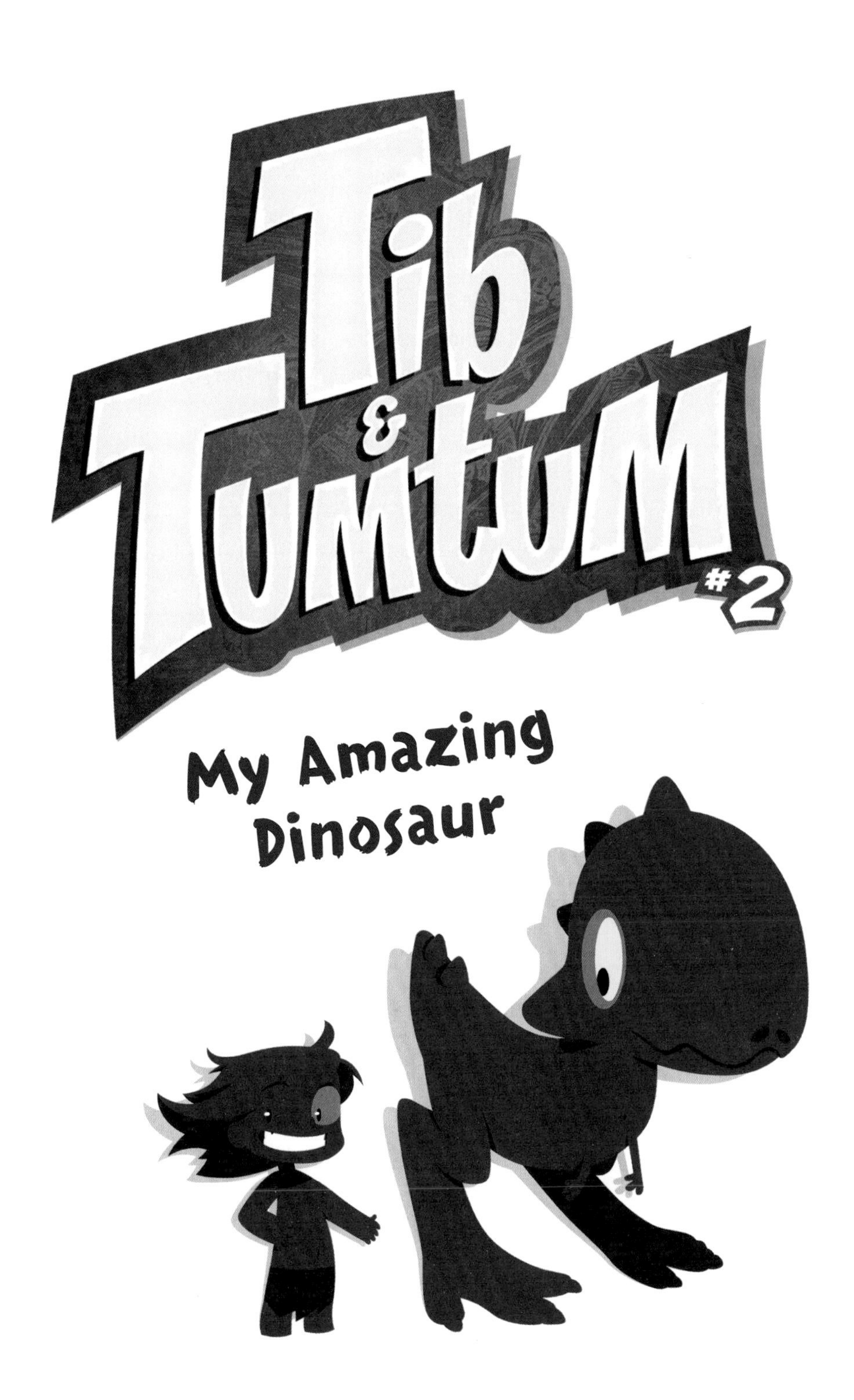

story
Grimaldi

art
Bannister

colors
Grimaldi

Graphic Universe™ • Minneapolis

For Papa.
Thank you to all my friends--girls, boys, cats, chickens, hairy, feathered, scaly, winged. I love you all very much.
--Grimaldi

Thanks to Jean-Claude, Anne, Eric, and Carol.
And of course, thanks to Flora, for all that there is in this book and author.
--Bannister

Story by Grimaldi
Art by Bannister
Coloring by Grimaldi

Translation by Carol Klio Burrell

First American edition published in 2014 by Graphic Universe™.

Graphic Universe™
A division of Lerner Publishing Group, Inc.
241 First Avenue North
Minneapolis, MN 55401 USA

For reading levels and more information, look up this title at www.lernerbooks.com.

Library of Congress Cataloging-in-Publication Data

Grimaldi, 1975-
[Mon dinosaure a du talent! English]
My amazing dinosaur / by Grimaldi ; illustrated by Bannister ; translation by Carol Klio Burrell. — First American edition.
p. cm. — (Tib & Tumtum ; #2)
Summary: Tib and his dinosaur friend Tumtum are back for more prehistoric (mis)adventures in the second installment of the Tib & Tumtum series.
ISBN 978-1-4677-1298-9 (lib. bdg. : alk. paper)
ISBN 978-1-4677-2427-2 (eBook)
1. Graphic novels. [1. Graphic novels. 2. Prehistoric peoples—Fiction. 3. Dinosaurs—Fiction.]
I. Bannister, illustrator. II. Burrell, Carol Klio, translator. III. Title.
PZ7.7.G758My 2014
741.5'315—dc23 2013036088

Manufactured in the United States of America
1 - BP - 12/31/2013

Everybody follow me to the big oak tree!

Come on! Everyone knows you exist now. So I might as well introduce you to the other kids.

Oof! Let's go! They're going to love you!

Hey, where did they all go?

Well... Lud said he wasn't interested. Nob and Jil were scared, I think. My papa needed to talk to my sister, and I think I'm going to go too...

They don't know what they're missing!

Lara!

Tara!

Kara!

My three girls! All accounted for!

Your mom and I want to know how you feel about there being a dinosaur in our forest.

I couldn't care less!
All animals have a right to live in peace, and the forest belongs to everyone!
Well said, my girl!
How about you, Kara? Nothing to say?

I'd like it better if Tib weren't friends with him.

My little girl is jealous because she's in loooove with Tib!
No way! No way!

Tib!
Yes?

Our parents talked to us about the dinosaur.

His name is Tumtum!

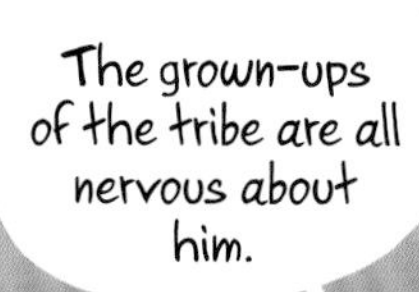

The grown-ups of the tribe are all nervous about him.
They told us not to go near him!

Plus, we have to tell them if we ever see him get too close to the tribe.
So there's no way you can bring him back here again!

The chief said he can stay!

Yes, but far away from the tribe! Otherwise, we're going to tell on you!
We'll be watching you!

Hmm...

I don't think you're in a lot of danger.

Don't go so fast, polka-dot face, or you'll fall down!

I'll do what I want!
FRT
FRT
FRT

Oh yeah? Well, you won't be bringing that dinosaur anywhere near our camp!

My dad's right!
Who knows what harm that nasty beast might do...?

At first, he scared me a lot.
But then I realized that your dinosaur is very handsome.
I totally agree with you, ma'am!

Your mom is a lot nicer than you are!
Pfffft!

That red hide would make a lovely dress!
Aha! That's the mom I know!

There he is!

Hee hee! He didn't hear me.

The saber-toothed tiger has spotted his prey.

More silent than a breeze!

Sneakier than a snake!

YAAHH!

SLURP

Uggh...
I like you too.

Where's Tib?
He went to the forest.

Probably looking for that dinosaur again...
Tom, we need to talk about his safety.

I thought he was playing with an imaginary friend. But in fact, he was with a dangerous animal!
What you call a dangerous animal saved his life.

I'd prefer it if he was just imaginary. Everybody's had an imaginary friend.
Oh boy, I had lots! And they were all amazing!

Mine was like a big brother. He was handsome, he was smart, he had dreamy eyes.
We were always together.
He listened to me, he cheered me up, he understood me. He made me feel brave!
He helped me be a better person!

He was just like me, right?

Yes, just like you.
Nice! We should talk about Tib's safety more often.

Oooh! Your new dress is magnificent!
And so original!
Hee hee! Thank you. These ideas just come naturally to me.

What are you making, Mama?
I can make fancy clothes just like Fili!

What do you think?
It's...special.
It's pretty gross.

Boohoo! I'm horrible at designing clothes!
No, you're not! The clothes you usually make are very nice!

Poor Mama...but it's really awful.

What if...with a little bit of berry juice...

Hey, look, Tumtum! I'm a dinosaur just like you!

Mama made a scene because I ruined her new dress. But she's the one who threw it away!

I'm going to bring her some plums. That'll make her feel better.

Hmm...

Hmm...

This one isn't ripe enough!

Poc

Poc

Poc

I guess you're just moral support! You get to play while I work!

Let's see how you do with two!

Now with three!

SHLAP
TOK

How about twelve?!

The difference between humans and animals is that humans get bored faster.

Hmm...

Mali, I'm going to take a little walk.
All right! Toodle-oo!

Ah, there it is!

Off we go!

TAK

CAW CAW
Pardon me!

SHPOF

Hee hee! Not bad for an old man.
Just in time!
Come on! Let's go see if there are any berries in the clearing!

There's a great view from up there.

Don't get too comfortable! I'll find you sooner or later!

All right, I've seen enough.

Is the chief back from his walk?
Yes, but he's taking a nap.

Poor old chief! A little walk tires him out!

GRT
GRT
GRT
GRT
GRT

GRRTTGRRTGRRTT

BLAM
BLAM
CRAAK

BONK
BONK
Stop that, Tumtum!
What are you doing?!

Oh, I see the problem.

Don't move. I'll get it off.
I have to pinch it and twist.
SNNFLE

RRRRHHHHHHH

I wonder if your ancestors got as worked up as you by a tiny little tick.

That's so beautiful!

That was worth staying for, but now I have to go home.

Good night, Tumtum!

Huff puff...

Arrgh...

Hey, look! Polka-dot face is afraid of the dark!
Puff huff...

The dark? No.

My mother, yes.
How many times have I told you to get home before sundown?!
You don't know how worried I've been!

PEEEP PEEEEEEP
PIP PEEP
PIP
PEEEP
PIP
PEEEP
PIP
PIP
PEEEP PIP PIP

PEEEEEEEEP
PEEEP

BOING
PEEP

BOING
PEEEEP

PEEP
THUNK!

PEEEEP

ZWIP!
PEEEEP

Ugh, what a horrible way to go!
SLRP
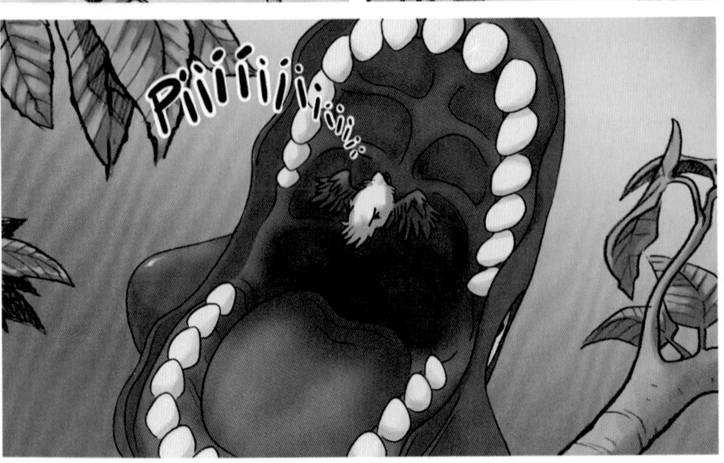
Piiiiiiiiii

And then the little bird fell into Tumtum's mouth.
We're so bored of your stories about your dinosaur!
Come see! I found an awesome tree for climbing over there!

See what I mean?
This tree is great! The branches are just the right height.
Can I climb up too?

Sorry, all full.

Why not go play with your monster?!

Yeah, you're right. I think he's close by. So be careful not to fall out of the tree!

Or he'll mistake you for a little bird...

No pushing!
Eeek!
I want down!

Tib! Come here for a moment.
Yes, Mama!

I'd like to talk to you about the dinosaur.
How come? What is it?

He's a big, dangerous animal.
No way! He's nice!

I'd rather decide that for myself.

So it would be good if you take me with you the next time you go to see him.

I'll watch how you play together, and I'll make sure for myself that you aren't in any danger.

Do you have anything to add, dear?
Not at all! What a good idea!

Either Papa's gone crazy, or he doesn't think it's such a good idea for Mama to see you.

Ha ha!
Here we go,
Tumtum!

Rats!
Mama's
following
me!

Hurry, let's hide! My mother's coming,
and I don't think she's going to like
seeing us together!

I thought for
sure that he
was around
here.

I can't do that every
time. We need to find
another solution.

I really want my mother to see that Tumtum isn't dangerous.
Sure, but that's impossible.

How can I show his nice side...?

I have an idea!

Help me! We need to pick lots and lots of flowers!
Your idea seems a little silly. But all right. It's true that Mama loves flowers.

Kara, you have to come help me!
Um, no thanks. I'll stay here to see how it looks from a distance.

Well?

No, he's still too scary. Put on more flowers!

There! That's perfect!

SLURP

MUNCH
MUNCH

WAAAAAAHH!
All those pretty flowers!
Aw, stop crying! That was a pretty bad idea, anyway.

Ha ha ha!

I need to wash off before I go home, or Mama's going to be mad.

Oh! I've covered up my face.

Wow, that's so great! With all the mud, no one can see my birthmark. I'm going to keep it on.

Look, Tib seems pleased with himself.
How classy.
Look at me! I don't have a birthmark anymore!

It does make it look that way.

But it's starting to itch a little.
You're not allergic, are you?

Aaah!
It itches so much!
Gotta wash off the mud!

Humph. That was another bad idea.
But look, it worked! With your face all red, we can't see your spot at all!

Here we go, Tumtum!
Tib! Where are you going?

Um...I'm going to collect some branches for the fire.
Oh, that's very nice of you.

Hmm...
Kwini! Come look! Right away!
I need your opinion about my new clothing creations.

Whew! Mama isn't trying to follow me again.

Yum. Thish ish very delicious.

Ready or not, here I come!

Look at those ants! They're taking leaves back to their home.

Hmm...Wasn't I supposed to bring back something too...?

Argh! I forgot to collect branches. Mama's going to know I wasn't telling the truth.

Hurry! Wood! Wood!

Raaah!
There aren't any branches lying around anywhere!

This is all I can find.
Waaaah.

Huh?!
What's he doing?

CRASH

It's really useful to have a dinosaur for a friend.

Today we're playing tag!

You're it! Ha ha ha!

He must be around here...

AAAAH!
Oops...

AAAAH!
Mama!
POF

Mama! Mama! Wake up! I'm fine. We were just playing!

Ma...
Wait, no! Tumtum! Stop!

I don't think waking her up like that is going to help our case.

You absolutely may not play with that dinosaur again!
But Maaama...

What's going on?
Waaah...

It turns out that our son is spending all his time with the dinosaur!
Oh, really? That's nice.

What's that?
With the dinosaur, our son is safe!
You really think that?

That critter has the strongest hind paws I've ever seen!
He can smash anything he wants with 'em.

His mouth is so big, a whole wolf could fit inside. And his teeth! Oh boy, those teeth!

There's no chance another predator will get near such a terribly terrifying animal!
Tib! You are forbidden to see that dinosaur again!
Ever!

Thanks a lot, Papa!
But I thought I was helping...
I've got my eye on you!

Can Tib come play with me?
That's a wonderful idea!

Go on! And have lots of fun!
But Mamaaaaa...

Let's pick some reeds.
You always make me do dumb things!

Look. I bend a bunch in two, and I tie a knot around it.

Just leave a few stems out on each side for arms, and that's how you make a person!

Hey, that gives me an idea!

La de da! The little boy and the little girl are going on a walk by the river.

And the dinosaur jumps on them and eats them!
GROAAR!

Waaaah!
Wow, I can't ever do anything fun with you!

If you're bored playing with Kara, go play with the kids your own age!
They're all mean.

You're exaggerating. They're over there. Go join them!

Hey, look! It's Tib!
Hey! Come with us!

You're just in time!
We missed you!
It's so nice to see you!
Huh?

Have lots of fun!
Tib was worrying over nothing.

We've been so bored today. But now that you're here, we can have fun.
Yeah! It's been a long time since we've played that.
Played what?

Played "Tib has a spot because..."!

Tib has a spot because Mother Nature wanted to point out the ugliest kid!
Tib has a spot because he scratches his eye all the time!
Tib has a spot because...
I thought all that enthusiasm was weird.

Mama! They won't stop making fun of my face!

Oh, dear! Maybe you should talk with them. Try to tell them that everyone looks different.
I have tried!

Try again, and be persistent!
Easy for you to say...

Oh, dear. Children care too much about how we look.
It's only when we grow up that we understand that looks aren't important.

Uh, pardon me, Kwini, but looks are very important! It's natural to be attracted to pretty things.
True, and you can't blame our kids for being repulsed by your son's birthmark.
That's unfair! I thought you'd have a more open mind.

I have a very open mind! Here's the proof: I've always accepted Mona as a friend in spite of her looks.
What?! What do you mean, my looks?!

Oh, that was just as an example. But you do know you're very big.
What?! You're so skinny I can see your bones!

Ha! You're just jealous!
Me, jealous of a bag of bones?! No way!
I'm starting to understand where our kids get their ideas from.

You again?
Uh... can I play with you, maybe?

Sure. If you want to play "Tib has a spot because" again.
Um, no!

Then go away!
We don't need you here.

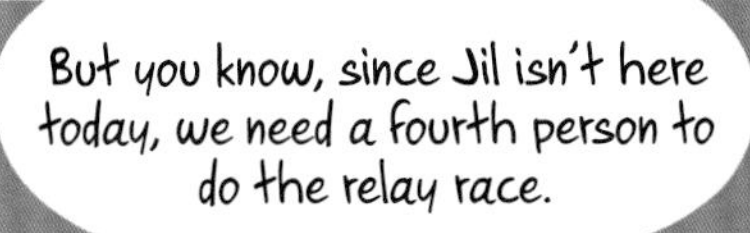
But you know, since Jil isn't here today, we need a fourth person to do the relay race.

Are you kidding? He's too clumsy!

Yeah, why don't you go play with your monster?
Tumtum isn't a monster! In fact, I'd rather go be with him!

But my mother would rather I play with you.
Aha! You see? He doesn't want to join us at all!
His mother is making him!

Aw, come on! Be nice!
We can try, just for today.
I don't care. You two do what you want.

But but but... if we let Tib into our gang, we won't be cool anymore!
And after that, anything could happen!

Oh, Tib's here! Can I play with you?
That's it! That's what I mean.

All right, if you really want to play with us, you have to pass the test.

Oh, yeah! That'll be fun!

Great idea!

But of course, if you fail, you must always play alone.
I get it.

What should we choose for the test?
How about a race against Tara?
Sure!
No, that's not fair! You run the fastest of everybody!

You have to run to the tree, go around it, come back here, and touch the stump.

It's not fair!
Get ready!
Get set!

GO!

What are you doing?
I'm giving him a head start. It's only fair, considering how good I am.

Aarrgh! You and your sense of fair play!
Now I can go!
Yaayyy! Thanks, big sister!

Yaayyy! Tib is first around the tree!
Go, Tara, go!

Huff! Puff! She's already right behind me. I'll never make it.

Arrgh!

Whoops!
THUMP

Watch ouuuut!
BOP

BONK

He touched the stump! He wins!
That doesn't count. He fell!
Nope, it counts. I admit defeat.
All right, he won...

...the first test out of two total.
I figured there'd be something like that.

For the second test, you have to climb all the way up that cliff.
What?! But that's impossible!

It's way too dangerous! Are you trying to get Tib hurt?!

She's right. I've never even gotten past where the rock hangs over.
If he falls off, he'll break all his bones.
Don't be silly! He'll never get that high.
He'll give up before that, and we'll be rid of him.

Looks like the easiest thing is for you to give up now, if you're scared.
I'm not scared!
I can do it!

You're completely crazy! I'm going to tell his parents!
Come back here, tattletale!

Be very careful.
Always try to keep three points of support.

The things I do to make my mother happy!

He's doing well, actually.
Hmph.

Whew! So far, so good.

But how am I going to get around the part that sticks out? It's going to be hard to hang on with my legs.

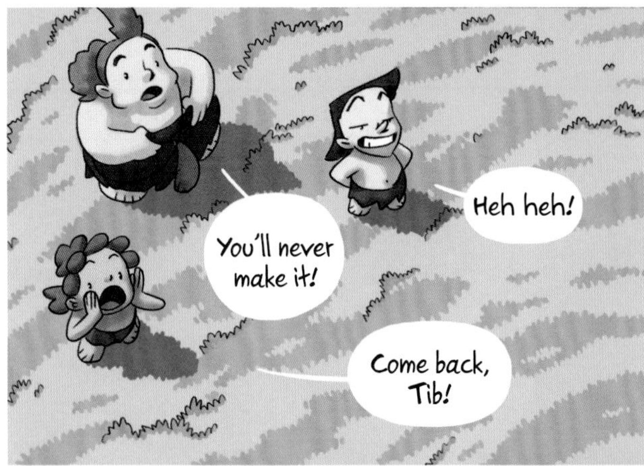
Heh heh!
You'll never make it!
Come back, Tib!

Umph!

He's crazy!

FRITCH
Ow!

AAAAAHHH

AAAHHH!

If he falls, he's done for!
If his parents find out, we're done for!

There they are!
Where's Tib?!

Up there.

Mama! Papa! Help!

Hold on! I'm coming to get you!

FRTCH
I'm slipping...

My little baby!

CRAK
CRAK
AAAHH!!

EEEEE!
CRASH
TUM TUM
TUM

TUM

CRAK

GRAOMF

POF

SPLUURTCH

My baby!
You scared the daylights out of us!
I don't feel so good...

Mama? This proves Tumtum is my friend, doesn't it? Can I play with him again?
Um, I don't know...

Come on, Kwini! How many times does that dinosaur have to save our son before you trust him?

Trust a wild animal? That seems ridiculous, but...

All right.
You can play with him again.
Yippee!

A few days later...
Mama! Can I go play with Tumtum?
Oh, yes, sure, but, um, wait...

Can you shake out the blankets first, please?
Yes, Mama.

I'm done!

Oh no! Quick! What else can I make him do?!

Tib!
Can you help me pick some fruit?
POF

Caught in the act!
Oops...

I'll help your mother pick fruit. You can go.
Super! See you later!
Don't come home too late...

Whew!
We played so much, I'm all worn out!

Hey!
I have a great idea!

I'll climb up on your back.

And ta-da! You can carry me back to the camp like this!

Whooaaa!

SPLAT

Heeeeey!
I'm tired! If you're really my friend, you'll carry me!

Yeah, but that's not quite the same!

What?! Nob?!
You have a spot?!

You all have spots!!

That's great!
What's he talking about?
He's nuts, that's all!

So I can play with you now!
No way.

But why?!
Because we don't want you, no-spot face!

Aaaah!

Mama! I had a horrible nightmare!!

I didn't have a spot! Boohoohoo!
I'm not sure I understand...

I'm going to play in the forest.
Um, wait, wouldn't you rather...

Honey...
Yes... I know... I need to let him be.

But I'm still going to go talk to the chief.

I know that the dinosaur saved our son.
I'm not completely against Tib seeing him from time to time. But...
I would feel a little better if he spent less time with him.

Chief! I have a problem! I can't get my son interested in hunting! I don't know what to do!

Chief! We need to talk about the future of our tribe. Our skills just aren't the best around these parts!
Is this business about having contests between the tribes still bothering you?

Hey! I was here before you!
Actually, I was first!
Calm down! Calm down!

I have an idea that will make everyone happy.

Listen to me, everybody!
I've decided to start a Life Skills School!

It's time to try to improve how we pass on our knowledge.
Up until now, each person taught what he knew to his own children. From now on, we're going to group the children according to their age, and each adult will teach them whatever job they know how to do best.

I don't get it.
Me neither.
How will that work?

It's simple. Who is the best at tracking animals?

My husband, obviously!

Right, so it will be you, Lar, who teaches that skill to the children.

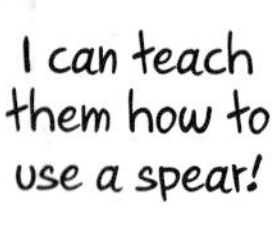
I can teach them how to use a spear!

Dressmaking!

Fishing!

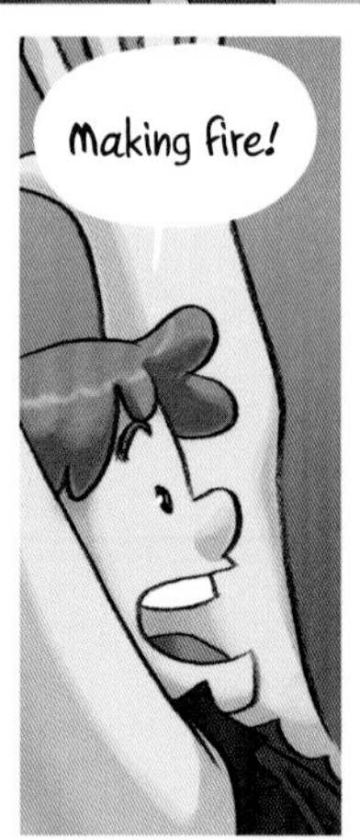
Making fire!

Our parents look like they're having fun up there.
Who cares? It's nothing to do with us!
C'mon, are you gonna throw your rock?!

Today I'm going to teach you how to make fire.
We'll go to a clear space, far from our tents or any bushes.
Follow me, everybody!
Yaaayyy!
Not you, Kara.

By whyyy?! I want to go to school too!
You can go next spring.
You're still too young.

Do you think this "school" thing is going to be good?
Sure! We're going to learn lots of things.

Anyway, if we're bored, we can always play "make fun of Tib."

Sir!
Tib's running away.
What?!

I don't know who first came up with this "school" idea, but he gets no thanks from me.
Waaah, I want to go!
Waaaah, I don't want to go!

There are two types of techniques for making fire: friction and percussion.

That sounds more complicated than I thought it would be.
How do you know all this?

Well, one day I was on a voyage far away from here! I had all my things in a sack, which was very heavy too.

I was walking peacefully through the forest, and I didn't notice that something was following in my tracks.
And guess what? It was a saber-toothed tiger!
Whoooaaaa!

I didn't even see him! All of a sudden he jumped on me from behind!
Luckily, at the last moment, I smelled him, and I threw my sack right at his head!
Wham!

Cool!

That's just what I'd have done!

Incredible!

You think that's incredible? Oh, but wait, this other time, I...
Papa, do you remember what you were supposed to be teaching us, originally?

Absolutely not! But give me a moment and I'll remember.

Are two flints enough to light a fire?
Yes, Tib?

No, you need at least one gold rock.

Yes, that's right. You need a piece of pyrite or marcasite.

Tib's such a teacher's pet!

You strike the flint against the marcasite to make a spark that lights the dry kindling.
TAK TAK TAK TAK TAK TAK TAK TAK

You pick up the grass.
You blow.
FFFFFF

And ta-da!
Hooray!
FLOOF

Now you try!
TAK TAK TAK TAK
TAK TAK TAK TAK
TAK TAK TAK

Help!
Tib's on fire!
What?! What?! Where?!

Oh, oops, sorry. I just thought your red spot was a fire.
Ha ha, very funny.

Tumtum! I have something neat to show you.

It's the greatest discovery of humans: how to make fire!

With fire, we can stay warm and cook our food. It's changed our lives!

Woohoo!
Look how pretty! This is progress!
FLOOF

Hey, where are you going?
Come back!
There's nothing to be scared of!

Oh, finally!
Where did you...?

PFFFFF

So I guess you don't like progress.

I'm going to teach you how to track animals.

My father is the expert.

We'll start by studying animal droppings.
Ha! You mean he's an expert in poo!

Quit laughing, you bunch of dopes! Identifying dung is an important part of studying animal tracks.
Tib got you this time.
Humph!

Look at this great one!
Bleccch!

It's weasel dung.
You can tell right away by its shape.
Are all droppings shaped differently?

Mostly, yes. The easiest to see is the difference between mammals, which make more solid dung, and birds, which make liquid droppings.

That's it! I know where Tib's spot came from!

One day Tib was looking at the sky. He got bird poo on his face, and because it was liquid, it spread all over.
Ha ha ha! Bleeeccch!

Look, this is hedgehog dung.

And that's from a boar.

Not only can we identify animals by their droppings, but we can also learn what they ate.
Oooooh.

Look at these fox droppings!

We can see tiny bones and also seeds from fruit.

The freshness of the dung lets us know if the animal passed by recently.
I wonder what Tumtum's droppings look like...

Regular deposits of droppings give us an idea of the animal's territory.
I've actually never seen him do his business.
But I hide to do it in private too.

I see there's already a bad student who isn't listening to everything I say.
I wonder if it looks like poo from other animals...

With all the berries you eat, your poo must be purple!

I'll pretend to go home.
See you tomorrow!

I'll have to spy on him to see him doing it.

Rats! He saw me!

Up in the trees will be a better hiding place.

Rats!

Rats again!

It's not easy to sneak up on a dinosaur!
I'm worn out! I need a little nap.

Hey, it's Tumtum! And he didn't see me!

He's just like us!
He covers up his business!

He's gone! I can finally see!

Hi! Was school good today?
Super!

Found one!

I was right! It's purple!
Ha ha ha! Cool!

Going to school makes you completely crazy!
THE END